TURKEY in the STRAW

Barbara Shook Hazen • *pictures by* Brad Sneed

Dial Books for Young Readers   New York

Published by Dial Books for Young Readers
A Division of Penguin Books USA Inc.
375 Hudson Street / New York, New York 10014

Text copyright © 1993 by Barbara Shook Hazen
Pictures copyright © 1993 by Bradley D. Sneed
All rights reserved
Printed in the U.S.A.
Designed by Jane Byers Bierhorst
First Edition
1 3 5 7 9 10 8 6 4 2

Library of Congress Cataloging in Publication Data

Hazen, Barbara Shook.
Turkey in the straw / by Barbara Shook Hazen
pictures by Brad Sneed.
p.   cm.
Summary / When things are looking bad, a farmer who would
rather fiddle than do his chores invites his neighbors to a
hoedown where he plays such a lively tune that his shy
daughter's pet turkey starts dancing, with happy results.
ISBN 0-8037-1298-7. — ISBN 0-8037-1299-5 (lib. bdg.)
[1. Fiddling — Fiction. 2. Farm life — Fiction.
3. Square dancing — Fiction.] I. Sneed, Brad, ill. II. Title.
PZ7.H314975Tu 1993 [E] — dc20 92-27516 CIP AC

The art for each picture is a watercolor painting,
scanner-separated and reproduced in full color.

Turkey in the Straw, according to Carl Sandburg, in his book
The American Songbag (Harcourt, Brace & Company, 1927), is
"the classical American rural tune…a song of the people…as
American as Andrew Jackson, Johnny Appleseed, and Corn-on-the-Cob….As a
song it smells of hay mows up over the barn dance floors, steps around like
an apple-faced farmhand, has the whiff of a river breeze when the catfish are
biting, and rolls along like a good wagon slicked up with new axlegrease."

Which set me wondering how it all got started, as well as
stirring up memories of my Ozark father.

B. S. H.

Once there was a farmer who was a born fiddler, and his wife who was a born worrier.

They had a daughter, Emmy Lou, who was shy and unsure what she was born to be.

How the farmer loved fiddling!
He fiddled in the morning instead of hoeing.
He fiddled at noon instead of haying.
He fiddled to the cows at sundown instead
of milking them.

Come on, little doggie, with a do-si-do.
Shake a leg, promenade, and away we go.

The farmer's fiddling made the wife fretful.

"Do something!" she'd nag. "If you don't stop your infernal fiddling, we're headed for the poorhouse, unless the gophers get us first, or the cows quit making milk, or there's a killer frost.

"Then what'll we do about Emmy Lou?"

Talk like this made the farmer fiddle faster and made Emmy Lou fidgety.

She'd tap her feet and twist her hair and pat her pet turkey gobbler, who seemed to understand.

One dismal day the gophers did come, and the cows quit making milk, and there was a killer frost.

The farmer did something all right. He saddled the mare, trotted to town, and posted a notice:

Come one, come all to a fiddling party at our place. Put on your dandy duds and your dancing shoes. Come for the fanciest fiddling this side of Fayetteville.

"Have you gone daft?" Emmy Lou's mother asked, irked, when he got back. "The cows are lolling around, the gophers are gnawing at the door, the money jar's bare as a baby's behind, our daughter's prospects are dim as a mouse-whisker moon. And all you have a mind to do is fiddle?"

"It's all I'm good at," the farmer fiddled up the gravel path. "You never know," he added, "some fine young man might hear my fiddling, and set his cap for Emmy Lou."

"Pie-in-the-sky fiddle-faddle!" the wife sniffed as Emmy Lou squirmed.

Still the good wife tried. She got fresh straw and gussied up the barn.

She gussied up Emmy Lou too. She starched her skirts, pinched her feet into secondhand party shoes, and ouched her hair in a high, tight braid.

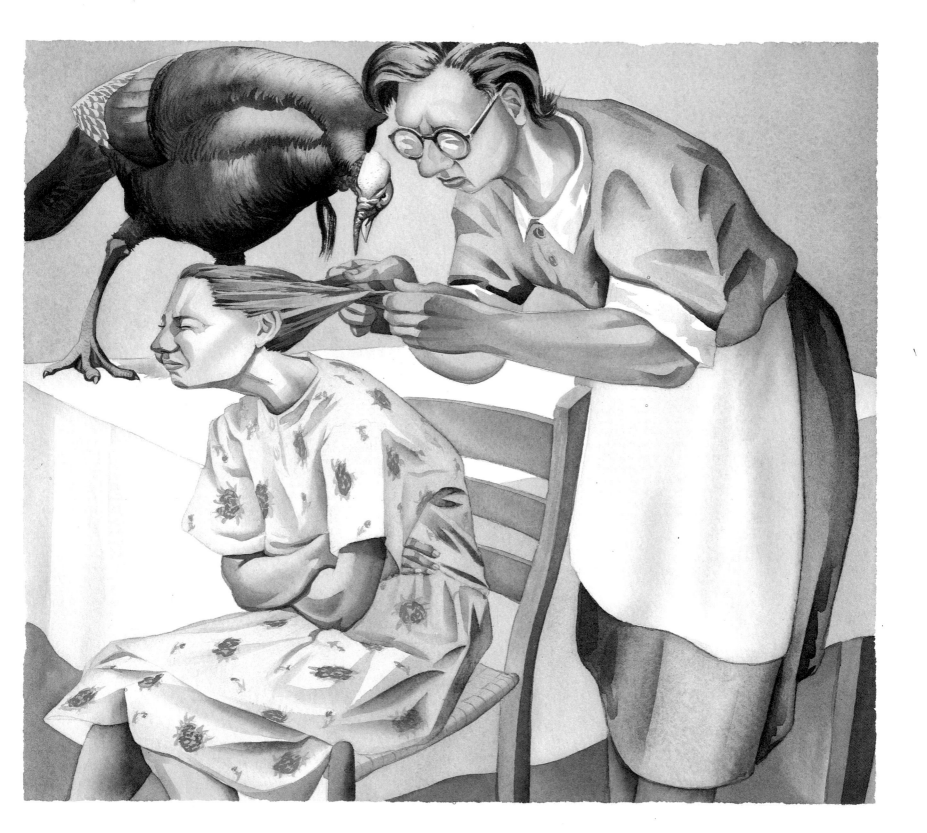

The guests came from miles around. The girls came in dimity dresses, and the boys in boots and red bandanas.

They came by wagon and horseback and shank's mare—except for one handsome, unsmiling stranger, who chugged up in his motor car, a Model T with big bug eyes.

Soon everyone was drinking cider, and making glad-to-see-you talk—everyone except Emmy Lou and the handsome, unsmiling stranger.

Soon after, the farmer started fiddling and everyone started square dancing—everyone except Emmy Lou and the handsome, unsmiling stranger.

Emmy Lou's father fiddled up a storm—

Down to the berry patch, do-si-do.
Swing your partner and away you go.

Emmy Lou's mother fretted up a fever.
Nobody asked their daughter to dance. And
no wonder! Emmy Lou sat with fidgety feet
and a turkey on her lap.

The farmer gawked and fiddled faster. He fiddled so fast that Mrs. Addlepaddle, the lady librarian, lost her lace petticoat, and Addie Mae, the schoolmarm, fell bonnet-first into the rain barrel, and Reverend Worthy slipped on an apple peel, did a double back-flip, and landed on the gray mare's back without missing a beat.

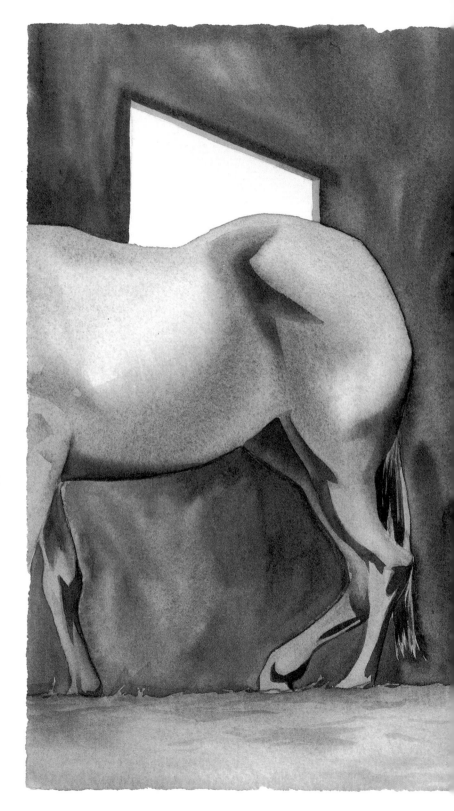

At the end of the first set the happy but tuckered-out guests sashayed to their seats.

The farmer tried out a new, still perkier tune.

And Emmy Lou's pet turkey strutted out onto the straw.

The turkey bobbed its head, and started lifting its feet—waddles wagging, feathers flapping—in time to the music.

The mother gasped. The farmer hoo-hahed. Emmy Lou giggled and forgot she was shy.

She got up, let down her hair, and kicked off her shoes, as she bowed to her partner, to the turkey in the straw.

The two of them did the fanciest dancing ever seen this side of Fayetteville.

At one point Emmy Lou got carried away, promenaded over to the stranger, and asked him to dance.

"I'd been hankering to meet you," he accepted shyly, "but I didn't know how."

It was a sight for worry-sore eyes.

It was also the beginning of better times
for the father, who gave up farming, and
the mother, who gave up fretting…

and for Emmy Lou, who gave up fidgeting
to exploring new possibilities of all that
she might be.